"*A Christmas Welcome* ... time for miracles."

—Ric...

Bestselling Author

"*The Christmas Welcome Sign* is another sweet and simple, yet provocative, story from author Dejah Edwards. Edwards has a knack for gently carrying readers along as her story unfolds, then climaxes the story with an almost unspoken personal call to those same readers to draw closer to the one who gave us all the original Christmas welcome sign. Enjoy this read, then pass it on to others to enjoy as well. They will thank you for doing so."

—Kathi Macias (www.KathiMacias.com)
Award-winning author of more than fifty books,
including the 2011 Golden Scrolls Novel of the Year,
Red Ink, and multiple Christmas stories

"A moving tale of a daughter losing her way, a mother's unrelenting love, and how prayer can lead a prodigal home."

—James C. Magruder, author of *The Glimpse*,
an inspiring story of forgiveness and reconciliation
between a father and a son. His nonfiction articles have
appeared in ten *Chicken Soup for the Soul* books

"The author tells a compelling story that has all the elements of a modern prodigal son. Mandy, the central character, reminds us that a planted seed is never too far away from blossoming."

—Pastor Joyce Villalobos, Oak Valley Church,
Yucaipa, California

"This book is another entertaining read by Dejah Edwards. But not only is it fun and easy to read, it also teaches you how to stay strong in the midst of both heartache and temptation. I recommend this book to everyone and especially to young women. It's a beautiful story that's just in time for Christmas!"

—Dee Hiemstra, former co-pastor and worship leader at Living Hope Fellowship, Rialto, CA

"*The Christmas Welcome Sign* is a beautiful story of restoration and the love of a mother and daughter. Dejah Edwards writes a story that warms your heart and reminds you to keep believing. Jesus always gives our story a new beginning."

—Pastor Teresa Hoffman, Christian Faith Center, Big Bear Lake, California

THE CHRISTMAS
WELCOME SIGN

Dejah Edwards

RIVER BIRCH PRESS

Daphne, Alabama

ISBN 978-1-956365-39-9 (print)
ISBN 978-1-956365-40-5 (e-book)

For Worldwide Distribution
Printed in the U.S.A.

River Birch Press
P.O. Box 868, Daphne, AL 36526

Dedicated to

The memory of Noel—named after Christmas—
my favorite time of the year. You made the last thirteen
Christmases special, making our house a home.
You were our beautiful sable collie with big brown eyes,
always loving and loyal. God truly gave part of Himself
when He made a dog—unconditional love.
I loved you your whole life. I'll miss you
the rest of mine.

═1═

When Allie pressed her forehead against the icy window to view the new fallen snow, a chill shot down her spine, but it didn't compare to the numbing cold that engulfed her heart. *Another year. Another Christmas without her.* She brushed away a tear. The blinking colored lights danced on the window pane. Allie turned around and walked to the tree. Hope impelled her to decorate it one more year. *Maybe this is the year she'll come home.*

Shivering she tossed some oak logs and pine cones into the wood stove then fixed herself a cup of Christmas blend tea. Soaking in the scents of cinnamon and cloves she set the teacup down and moved her chair closer to the tree. Allie fingered the delicate pink ballerina ornament—Clara from *The Nutcracker*. Images flooded her mind of Mandy twirling around at a ballet recital. How she loved her ballet class! Allie had a hard time getting her to take off her tutu. Allie's thoughts traveled back to the look on Mandy's face when she opened the present containing the Clara ornament and cried, "Oh, Mom, I love it!"

She tenderly caressed another ornament, this one of the TV Lassie. It resembled the first collie puppy she gave Mandy one Christmas. Mandy adored her blue-eyed bundle of fur whom she also named Lassie. And they became inseparable friends.

Allie's eyes welled up when she gently touched the "It's A Wonderful Life" ornament. Visions danced in her mind of

1

cuddling with Mandy on the couch—butter from the popcorn dripping down their arms—watching their favorite Christmas movie.

A slight smile formed on Allie's face when the Rudolph ornament's nose lit up. She recalled how Mandy would giggle every time the light in the nose flashed red. Allie turned away from the tree. *Enough memories for today.* She was sure the hole in her heart grew bigger each day.

Allie opened her Bible, and started reading in the book of Jeremiah. A great feeling of peace swept into her heart. Then she journaled her daily prayers to God, a practice that gave her peace and increased her faith and hope.

Allie wrote in her prayer journal:

Lord, you promised me in the book of Jeremiah You will give our children a heart to know You and they will return to You with their whole heart. You know my heart, and You hear my prayers. You care about all that concerns us. Help me to remember that You love my daughter more than I ever could. Help me to be strong and trust You. Thank You for Your great love for me.

Allie placed her Bible on the shelf and stood up just when the phone rang.

"Hi Allie. What are you doing?"

"Just about to fix another cup of tea."

"Listen, Sis. Ben and I really want you to come to our home for Christmas."

"Thanks for the invitation, but I think I'm staying here."

"Hey, if the snow gets too bad, Ben and I could drive up the mountain and come and get you."

"That's very thoughtful of you, Amy, but I'm fine here."

"We don't want you to be alone. No one should be alone at Christmas."

"I'm not alone. My friend Carol and I will be going to the play at our church on Christmas Eve. Remember the spinach pie you taught me to make? I'm bringing that for the potluck afterwards."

"All right, dear sister, please enjoy your Christmas. See you on New Year's. We'll bring your presents then."

"Thanks, Amy. See you soon."

⚊2⚊

Allison "Allie" Andrews was born in Kalispell, Montana. Her parents moved to southern California when her dad was offered a full professorship at UCLA. Allie was everyone's sweetheart. Her bright smile and her kindness easily won her friends. Her big espresso-brown eyes, sandy-blonde hair, and her sleek frame typified a California girl. She looked like she could be on the cover of a Beach Boy's album.

Allie enrolled at UCLA to obtain a Bachelor of Science in accounting. It was here where she met Luke Morrison one night, while studying at the university library. Allie had the strangest impression someone was staring at her. She looked up. Blinked twice.

"Hi, my name is Luke Morrison. Would it be all right if I sat down?"

Her cheeks grew hot. She extended her hand and giggled. "Pleased to meet you too. I'm Allison Andrews. Everyone calls me Allie."

Immediately she was charmed by Luke. The first thing she noticed about him was the Kirk Douglas dimple on his chin. His sandy-blond hair fell over his deep-set arctic-blue eyes. He was about six feet tall with broad shoulders like someone who paddled an outrigger canoe.

"I noticed you were reading *To Kill A Mockingbird*," Luke observed. "It's one of my favorites. Is it assigned reading for one of your classes?"

"Oh no, reading a novel is how I take a break from studying accounting."

He grinned. "Sounds like a great plan. Don't you love Harper Lee and how she weaves the book's title into the story?"

"Yes, I do. Do you like to read?"

"Guilty as charged."

She raised her eyebrows. "That's interesting. Most boys don't like to read—unless it's a school assignment."

"Well, Allie, I love to read."

Allie smiled. "What's your major?"

"Math. Yours is accounting?"

She nodded. "Yes, accounting is my major."

It was his turn to raise his eyebrows. "Wow, smart girl."

Allie laughed. Luke made her feel comfortable.

"My plans are to teach high school math in my hometown," he said. "First, I feel it's my obligation to join the Marines. With a four-year degree I can bypass general enlistment and move directly into officer training. I'll sign up for the special two-year program."

Luke was easy to talk to. Allie soon discovered he grew up in Big Bear Lake, a quaint mountain town. His dad was a pediatrician. His mother a cardiac nurse. What impressed her the most was Luke openly professed he was a Christian.

"I love God with all my heart," he declared, "and someday when I teach, I hope to start a Christian club. My desire is to lead young people into a relationship with Jesus."

From that moment on, they were inseparable. Luke's family fell in love with Allie, and Allie's parents adored Luke. Two years later they became man and wife. Luke loved his country and, as planned, joined the Marines. A year later their daughter Mandy was born. Sadly Luke was killed in Afghanistan when Mandy was only three years old. He was one of the Marine officers deployed to Afghanistan after the 9-11 attack on the Twin Towers.

Allie had been sitting on the floor playing blocks with Mandy when she noticed an official sedan pull into her driveway. She watched from the window as two men in full-dress uniforms slowly walked up the porch steps. She hung onto the wall for support and held her breath. The doorbell rang.

"Go play with your dolls, Mandy. I have to talk to these men."

"Okay, Mommy."

Allie opened the door. One look at the man's face and she feared the worst.

"Mrs. Morrison, I'm Sergeant McManus and this is Chaplain Ray. I'm sorry to have to bring you this news, but your husband, Luke, was killed in action. He was a very brave man. He saved most of his men during a raid. Is there anyone we can call for you?"

Allie's hands flew to her mouth. The room started spinning.

The notification officer grabbed Allie just before she fainted. "Mrs. Morrison, come lie down on the couch."

The chaplain rushed into the kitchen. He returned with a cold towel, which he placed on Allie's head.

"No, no it can't be. Oh God, no!" Allie screamed and trembled violently.

"I'm afraid she's going into shock," Sergeant McManus informed Chaplain Ray.

The chaplain held up a piece of paper. "I found this church bulletin on the kitchen counter. I'll phone the pastor."

A small, frightened looking girl entered the room, speaking first to Allie and then to the officer. "Mommy, what's wrong? What's wrong with my mommy?" Tears rolled down the scared child's face.

The chaplain gathered Mandy in his arms. "Your mommy

6

will be all right. Some of your friends from church are coming over to help. What's your name?"

"Amanda Joy Morrison. Everyone calls me Mandy. I'm three years and a half years old."

In less than thirty minutes, Pastor Tom and several people from the church showed up with food as well as toys for Mandy. Allie's closest friend, Carol, ran through the front door and held Allie. Her husband, Patrick, Luke's best friend, had tears in his eyes. He and Carol were like family to Allie and Luke. They did everything together.

———○———

Since that heartbreaking time so many years ago, Allie had done all she could to be both a mother and father to Mandy, who had turned into a beautiful young woman. Her thick auburn hair cascaded down her back. Her eyes were the color of jade, and her porcelain skin gave her an exotic look. Not only was she sweet and caring but always had a kind word for everyone. Her smile lit up a room. Her passion was volunteering at the children's hospital with their dog, Bear. She loved to make the children laugh when Bear performed his many tricks.

Her dream—to become a lawyer and fight crimes against children. She wanted to go to USC and major in political science and then go on to law school there. Unlike many teenagers, she had a deep compassion for others. In her junior year of high school, she accompanied other youth to Mexico to help build an orphanage.

═ 3 ═

Logan Walker enrolled in Big Bear High School in Mandy's senior year. He and Mandy had the same Advanced Algebra class. He walked in and glanced around the room. When he saw Mandy he quickly took the empty seat next to her. In his mind, the closeness would work its magic. Soon there would be a friendship or hopefully a romantic relationship. All he knew is that he must get to know this beauty.

Logan was tall with beach-boy blond hair and broad shoulders. His cornflower-blue eyes and perfectly set dimples soon won him the place as the most popular guy on campus. He soon became the football quarterback. Every girl in the high school had a crush on him.

Everyone but Mandy. She was too busy on the debate team and track team. She believed running increased her brain power. Mandy was smart and sensitive. Logan in contrast was a self-centered live-for-the-moment kind of guy. He did all he could to get Mandy's attention. His lack of interest in the things of God made Mandy shy away from him.

Logan soon devised a plan. He showed up at the Christian club she attended. In an attempt to show himself smarter than the leader, he asked philosophical questions to try and contradict him. His actions infuriated Mandy. In the hallway after one of the meetings, she walked right up to him and declared, "You are a real jerk. Did you just come to the Christian club to mock us?"

Realizing this could ruin his chances with her, he softened his approach.

"I'm so sorry. You're right. I guess I get defensive when I don't understand things. I really am interested in learning more about the Bible. Please, forgive me."

"Hmm." Mandy tossed her head and started to walk away.

Logan ran after her and grabbed her arm. "I'm serious, Mandy."

Shaking his arm loose, she said, "Logan Walker, don't think your charm will work on me. I see right through your schemes."

Logan threw his hands up as Mandy stormed away.

For the next several weeks, Mandy didn't even look at Logan when he came into her math class. He did put notes on her desk begging for forgiveness. Mandy just crumbled them up and threw them into the trash can on the way out of the room.

Her best friend, Maria, suggested, "Why don't you test him and invite him to church? See how he reacts. After all, we're supposed to forgive."

Mandy knew Maria was right. But the thought of spending time with Logan didn't appeal to her. Mandy wasn't sure if it was her conscience or her curiosity that got to her. After class one day, as Mandy gathered her books, she wasn't watching and bumped right into Logan.

"Oops, sorry."

"It's okay, Mandy. How are you doing?"

"Fine. Hey, would you like to go to church with me Sunday?"

"For real? Sure. What time? Should I meet you there?"

"It starts at ten o'clock. My church is Faith Community Church on Big Bear Boulevard. It's right near the Wendy's."

"I think I can find it. See you Sunday. Oh, what should I wear?"

"You can dress casual."

4

Allie had mixed feelings when Mandy told her she invited Logan to church. She and her daughter were close, so she was aware of the incident at the Christian club. She also knew Mandy was compassionate and often invited her unsaved friends to church.

Logan showed up Sunday right on time. He wore khaki pants and a Tommy Bahama shirt.

Mandy greeted him. "Hi, Logan. This is my mother, Allison Morrison."

"So pleased to meet you, Mrs. Morrison." He extended his hand.

"Nice to meet you too. I hope you enjoy the service." She noticed Logan smile one of his charming smiles and wink at Mandy. *I'm going to keep a keen eye on this one.*

Logan sat perfectly still and appeared to absorb every word the pastor shared. As they walked out of church, Logan turned to Allie. "Would you allow me to take Mandy to brunch? I'd love to discuss the sermon with her. You're welcome to come with us, Mrs. Morrison."

Allie hesitated. "No, I can't go with you. I have to get home. The nursery is delivering plants." She still did not trust Logan.

Mandy gave Allie a pleading look. "Mom, I promise to be home by two o'clock. I'll still have enough time to help you with planting before dinner."

Allie's lips tightened and she sighed. She still did not approve of Mandy spending time with Logan. "Logan, you have my daughter home on time."

11

"Yes, Ma'am." Logan smiled.

———•◦•———

At brunch Logan feigned interest in every word the pastor preached. He even listened intently when Mandy read aloud the scriptures the pastor alluded to. Logan, the master of manipulation, convinced Mandy that he wanted to know God. The idea of Logan desiring a relationship with God excited her because she had a part in it.

When Mandy arrived home she couldn't wait to share the news about Logan with her mother. Allie still was not convinced and warned Mandy to be careful. Allie's suspicions about Logan grew when she saw Mandy falling for him. At first, they only dated when he came over to the house or they met at church. Mandy always attempted to make their time together into a Bible study.

Allie's sharp eyes saw right through Logan. He focused more on Mandy than the Bible. He sat through the times Mandy read from the Bible, but he slowly maneuvered her to other things. First it was "Hey, let's go get some ice cream." Then one night he came over early and after about an hour suggested they meet some kids from school at the bowling alley. Logan devised plans to get Mandy out of the house and away from Allie.

═ 5 ═

One night after they went to a basketball game at the high school, Logan suggested they walk down to the lake. Mandy, trusting him, agreed. When they arrived Logan spread out a towel for them to sit on. Immediately he talked about the stars and God's creation and how beautiful it all was. He turned to Mandy. "Nothing is as beautiful as you. I think I am falling in love with you. God brought us together."

Mandy put her hand over her mouth. *Did he really mean these words?* A tingle went up her spine.

He leaned closer. "Would it be all right if I held you and gave you a little kiss? I want to show you how I feel."

All Mandy could do was nod her head.

Logan moved in. He wrapped his arms around her. Gently he tilted her face toward his. The kiss started slowly. Mandy felt as though she were falling. The kiss grew more intense. With her head spinning Mandy realized they were lying down, and Logan was almost on top of her. Shaking she pushed him off and sat up.

"What are you doing, Logan?"

"Oh, Mandy, I'm so sorry. I guess I got carried away. I promise this will never happen again."

"Take me home."

When Mandy walked through the door that night, Allie knew something was wrong. She kept pressing her, but Mandy replied that she was just tired and wanted to go right to sleep. She said she had cramps. Allie wasn't convinced. Her distrust and fear about Logan grew.

The next few weeks Logan didn't show up for church. When Allie inquired Mandy told her that he was in Idaho spending his Christmas vacation with his real dad. Relieved Allie now went ahead and planned holiday events, still worrying about how Mandy seemed distant since the last time she was with Logan.

≈6≈

Since Christmas was her favorite holiday, Mandy soon was her old self. Mom and daughter baked cookies, decorated the tree, and joined others from their church singing Christmas carols at the local nursing home.

Christmas morning Allie surprised Mandy with an Apple laptop computer.

Mandy threw her arms around Allie. "Mom, this is perfect! Just what I'll need next fall for college."

Mandy's gift to her mom was a small diamond tennis bracelet. She had saved her babysitting money all year for it.

The smile on Allie's face said it all. "I love it. I'll never take it off. I love you with all my heart."

"Love you more, Mom."

Mandy and Allie were inseparable during the holidays. Every day they found something fun to do. The day after Christmas, mother and daughter journeyed to the after-Christmas sales. One of their yearly rituals. They stocked up with gifts for next year. Allie found her greatest treasure at Hobby Lobby—a Christmas Welcome Sign. The sign read "All Hearts Come Home For Christmas." Under that phrase it read, "Welcome Home."

Allie told Mandy, "Look, I can hang this on the front porch. When you go away to college or no matter how far you roam, this sign will always welcome you home."

Mandy flew into her arms. "Oh, Mom, I love you so much!"

Allie cherished every moment with her daughter. Sadly

she knew next year Mandy would be away at college, and their relationship would be different.

7

On New Year's Eve, they grabbed chairs and walked down to the lake to watch the fireworks with the rest of the neighborhood. Mandy's phone kept ringing. She shut it off and sighed. It pinged with multiple texts. Allie looked over at Mandy. She seemed disinterested. Allie suspected it was Logan. She decided not to say anything because she did not want to spoil their time together. When they arrived home Mandy went into her room. Allie heard her shouting, "Just leave me alone. I told you I didn't want to see you anymore."

The next morning Mandy opened up to her mother. "I don't know why Logan doesn't get the message. I don't want a relationship now with him or anyone for that matter. I need to concentrate on getting myself ready for college. I really don't want to be mean to him, Mom. He's just relentless."

8

At church on Sunday the pastor spoke on forgiveness. "Sometimes when we forgive those who hurt us it can draw them to Christ."

Allie could tell that Mandy was listening intently.

On the way home she said, "Mom, you know I haven't been very kind to Logan. I'm his only Christian friend. Maybe I'm the one that's supposed to lead him to Christ."

"I think you tried that, Mandy. You befriended him and invited him to church."

"It's my fault he thought we were more than friends. I enjoyed the attention he gave me. I need to make it clear to him we can only be friends."

Allie knew Mandy had a heart of compassion. Yet she felt unsure of Logan's motives and did not trust him with her daughter.

The next day Mandy went into the village to shop for some new clothes. As she walked down the street, she thought she noticed Logan drive by in his car. Within minutes she heard someone calling her name.

"Hey, Mandy, wait up!"

Logan ran towards her. Mandy waited for him to speak first.

"Listen, Mandy, I'm so glad I ran into you. I've been try-ing to tell you how sorry I am."

"I accept your apology. Like I told you before, I don't

want any kind of relationship. My focus is on college in the fall."

"I understand, Mandy. Listen, after graduation I'm probably moving to Idaho with my dad. He wants to make me a partner in his construction business. Can't we just be friends? I could use a good friend. Actually I miss you reading the Bible to me."

"Well, I guess so."

Logan grinned. "Hey, I haven't asked anybody to the prom. Would you honor me and go with me as my friend? No strings attached."

Mandy softened. She always dreamed of her senior prom and what type of dress she would wear. So she agreed. "Okay, Logan. I'll be your date."

Logan and Mandy continued to casually date. He stopped pushing her. Mandy realized he was a lot of fun to be with. One of their favorite activities was going on Logan's stepdad's pontoon boat where Logan taught Mandy how to fish. She was thrilled every time she caught something.

=9=

Although Mandy saw Logan more like a brother/friend, Allie saw something different in Logan. He looked at Mandy like someone looks at an expensive car they'd like to own. Every time he was around Allie, he feigned politeness but evaded eye contact. He still attended church with Mandy but not on a regular basis. He always seemed to find some excuse on Sunday to miss church. Allie did not like this relationship. She noticed when Mandy wasn't with Logan she would spend hours on the phone with him.

Even her best friend, Maria, confided in Allie. "Mrs. Morrison, I'm worried about Mandy. She never hangs out with her friends anymore. She never talks about how she can't wait to go to USC. It's kind of like Logan has put a spell on her."

Maria's information confirmed Allie's concern. She knew it was time to confront her daughter, who had been avoiding her too.

When Mandy arrived home from school the next day, Allie said, "You got a minute?"

"Sure, Mom, what's up?"

"I'm worried about you. You say you and Logan are just friends, but I see the way he looks at you. You've abandoned all your old friends. It seems you only have time for him."

"Oh Mom, I'm just having fun. He's been a perfect gentleman. We really have a lot in common."

Allie sighed. *What could Mandy and Logan possibly have in common? They're as different as day and night.* "Please, be careful."

20

"Mom, you're being overprotective. It's really all right for me to have some fun before I go away to school."

Allie didn't know what to say. Mandy always listened to her in the past and never questioned her judgment. Allie didn't bring the subject up again. She just prayed for wisdom for Mandy. She believed the closer it got for her daughter to leave for college, the less of an interest she'd have in Logan.

⸻

Prom night was only two weeks away. Allie and Mandy went dress shopping. Allie picked out three styles that were colors that enhanced Mandy's beauty. Mandy chose a dress that made Allie's eyebrows raise.

"Oh no, Mandy, that one is much too revealing."

"Mom, you're old-fashioned."

Where is this coming from, thought Allie. Mandy always respected her mother's opinion. Finally, they agreed on a form-fitting mint green spaghetti-strap dress. It was a little too low-cut for Allie, but an improvement over the dress Mandy wanted.

⸻

A few days before the prom, Mandy announced, "After the prom Logan and another couple want to go to Six Flags Magic Mountain. They're staying open all night for graduates."

"No, absolutely not. I don't want you driving up or down the mountain in the dark."

"Logan rented a limousine. None of us will be driving. Logan's cousin doesn't live far from Magic Mountain, and he said we could spend the night there. He has a large home. Sandy and I will sleep in one room, and Logan and Tom in another."

"I do not want you staying at someone's home unchaperoned."

"Oh Mom, you just don't trust me!"

Mandy slammed the door and ran outside. Within minutes, Logan pulled up. She jumped into his car.

"I'm glad you texted me. Mandy, what's going on?"

"Mom doesn't want me spending the night at a stranger's house."

"She's just being a mom. I can have my aunt call her."

"I don't think it would make any difference. Once my mom makes up her mind, that settles it."

"I think it's hard on your mom without your dad, it just being you and her."

"I'm sure that's part of it. But it's my prom night. This only happens once in a lifetime. I just want to have some fun."

10

Prom night rolled around and Allie did not relent. Mandy knew she would have to defy her mother. Ever since the day she ran out of the house and slammed the door, their relationship had been strained.

Mandy looked lovely in her mint green prom dress, just the right color to enhance her jade green eyes. Logan arrived with a gardenia wrist corsage. Allie had all her cameras ready to take pictures of them before they left. Mandy rushed through the photos.

"We're sharing a limousine with Tom and Sandy. Tom's father hired a professional photographer to do a photo shoot for all four of us. We need to hurry and get there."

The last words Allie spoke were to Logan. "Take care of my daughter."

Mandy felt like a princess going to a ball as she climbed into the limousine.

Logan took Mandy by the hand. "Wow, you look beautiful."

Mandy blushed and squeezed his hand. She took a long look at Logan. She realized just how handsome he was. In his tuxedo he could very well be a model on the cover of *Gentlemen's Quarterly*. "You look very handsome."

He flashed her a winning smile. "Thanks! Tom's family lives on a lake. The photographer should get some awesome shots."

Logan put his arm around Mandy's waist when they arrived at Tom's.

Sandy looked lovely in her pale blue off-the-shoulder dress. The color made her blue eyes sparkle.

Sandy grabbed Mandy's arm. "We're going to have so much fun tonight." Mandy smiled. The photographer quickly staged several shots of the four of them. Next he took photos of the individual couples. Using the limo as a prop, one of the most fun pictures was of Logan lifting Mandy off the hood of the car. The timing for the photo shoot was perfect. The sun was just setting. They got great sunset pictures, even some silhouettes.

———◦———

The prom was held at an event center because it included a sit-down dinner. Everything was elegant—white linen tablecloths with vases of pink roses. After the dinner the chaperones moved the graduates into the ballroom for dancing. The theme for the prom was black and white. All the decorations, including the flooring and balloons, were done in black and white. It made everyone's dresses pop. To add to the fun, black and white ice cream was served.

At 1:30 a.m. Tom and Sandy insisted they leave. "We need to have enough time to enjoy Magic Mountain."

On the way down the mountain, Tom pulled a bottle from under the seat. "Let's celebrate, graduates!" He poured four glasses. When Mandy refused Logan assured her it was just champagne. "It'll help you have a great time."

Mandy relented. The bubbles tickled her nose. She did not like how it made her head feel. Mandy got even more uncomfortable at the way Tom's hands were all over Sandy. She didn't seem to mind. She enjoyed it. Mandy tried to look away.

They stopped at Logan's cousin's house first to change their clothes. Mandy had snuck shorts, a t-shirt, jacket, and tennis shoes out of the house a few days earlier.

They got back in the limo and headed for Magic Mountain. Tom pulled out a smaller bottle and offered it to them. This time Mandy put her hand up and shook her head. She noticed Logan wasn't refusing. Mandy and Logan rode every ride twice. He won a giant teddy bear for Mandy at one of the game booths. Tom and Sandy seemed to disappear.

⟨ 11 ⟩

At 5:00 a.m. Mandy said she was exhausted. Searching for Tom and Sandy, they found the limo driver. He pointed to the car, and Logan and Mandy headed towards it. When Logan opened the door, Tom and Sandy jumped up. Their clothes and hair were disheveled, and Sandy's make-up was a mess. She just laughed and shrugged her shoulders.

At Logan's cousin's house later, Logan asked Mandy, "Would you like something to eat?"

"That sounds good. How about some tea and toast?"

After they ate, Mandy went into the bathroom to wash and brush her teeth. She walked into the bedroom she was supposed to share with Sandy. She found Logan half asleep in a chair.

"What are you doing here? Where's Sandy?"

"I'm afraid she's in the room with Tom."

"Well, you're not staying in here."

"I was just going to lay down next to you and go to sleep."

"No, Logan, you need to go sleep on the couch."

Logan grunted something under his breath and stormed out. Mandy lay down. She wished she was in her own bed, yet part of her really enjoyed this night. She was all mixed up. She did not want Logan angry with her. *Was I just being childish?* Getting up, she tiptoed into the living room. Logan was lying on the couch with his eyes open.

"Logan, I came to check on you. I didn't mean to make you mad."

"It's okay, honey. Come sit down by me."

As soon as Mandy sat, Logan slipped his arms around her. His lips found hers. Her body melted into his. He started to caress her. At first she resisted. As Logan's kisses moved down her neck, she gave in. Just before they crossed the line, Mandy stopped him.

"Mandy, you're beautiful. I love you. I will never hurt you. You're all I want."

"We need to stop, Logan. This is something for the marriage bed."

She rose up and went back to her room. Lying there in the dark, she could still feel Logan's hands on her.

$\Longrightarrow$ 12 $\Longleftarrow$

Allie stayed up and prayed all night for her daughter's safety. At 3:00 a.m., after the prom had been over for more than an hour, she knew Mandy had disobeyed her and gone to Magic Mountain. She knew she needed to intercede for her daughter. In her prayer journal she wrote the following prayer from Psalm 91:

> Lord, I know my child's help (and protection) comes from You, the Lord who made heaven and earth. You will not let her foot be moved. You will not slumber. Thank You for being my child's keeper, You are the shade on my child's right hand. The sun will not strike my child by day, nor the moon by night. Thank You in advance for keeping my child from all evil. You will keep my child's life from this time forth and forevermore, amen.

Shortly after noon Mandy awakened to Tom shouting, "The limo's here. It's time to go get breakfast and head home."

Ashamed, her head down, Mandy walked into the living room. Tom and Sandy were laughing and teasing one another. Logan walked up and put his arm around her. "Good morning, babe. Did you sleep well?"

He kissed her on the cheek. Mandy stiffened and didn't look up at him. Although shame engulfed her, her desire for Logan was stronger. He awakened something in her she seemed to have no control over. He took her by the hand and led her to the limo. Inside he held her close.

They stopped for a quick pancake breakfast at IHOP, then headed up the mountain for home. The limo driver dropped Sandy off at Tom's house. Mandy's head throbbed and her body was beyond exhaustion. Still her main concern was what her mother would think of her defiance.

The limo pulled into Mandy's driveway. Logan jumped out to open the door for her. He started to walk her up the driveway. Fearing her mother's retaliation, she stopped him. "I can do this. Go home and get some rest."

He kissed her briefly on the lips. "I'll call you later."

<hr/>

Mandy went to the front door. It was unlocked. Walking in she saw her mother sitting at her desk with her Bible in her lap.

She ran to her, tears streaming down her face. "I'm sorry, Mom. So sorry."

Mandy realized she was not only apologizing for her disobedience but even more for what she allowed to happen with Logan.

Holding her daughter with tears in her eyes, Allie said, "I'm disappointed, Mandy, but I love you and always will. No matter what."

"Mom, I'm so tired. I'm going to shower and climb into bed."

"Okay. Get some rest. When you wake up I'll make us some dinner."

Standing in the shower Mandy let the hot water soothe her body. She wished she could scrub away her actions from the night before. Everything inside her told her it was wrong to allow Logan to fondle her like that. Yet her insides craved his touch. Climbing into bed Mandy tried to pray, but her thoughts were only of Logan.

≈ 13 ≈

While Mandy slept Allie prayed. Taking down her prayer journal from her desk, she wrote Joshua 1:9:

"Have I not commanded you? Be strong and courageous. Do not be afraid; do not be discouraged, for the Lord your God will be with you wherever you go."

She finished with a prayer:

Heavenly Father, I place Mandy in Your loving hands. Give her peace knowing that You are right by her side. Give her courage and wisdom to make right decisions. Keep her safe. Use her for Your glory.

Mandy woke up famished around 9:00 o'clock. Allie made her grilled cheese, pineapple sandwiches, and tomato soup. Her mother was a good caring mother. Mandy knew she was wrong. She made a promise to herself. *I will never deliberately disobey my mother again.* Would Mandy be able to keep that promise? Only time would tell.

Logan started a summer waiter job at a five-star restaurant. He seldom had Sundays off, so he rarely attended church. Mandy took a retail job in Big Bear Lake Village at one of the tourist shops. They promised to give her every other Sunday off. Although both had summer jobs, Mandy and Logan were together every chance they got. Mandy tried her hardest to keep Logan at a distance. She didn't want things to get out of control again.

≈14≈

One night several weeks later, after Logan and Mandy left the bowling alley, Logan parked down by the lake. "Close your eyes. I have a surprise for you."

Gently Logan pushed her hair away from her neck. She felt something around her neck. "All right, you can open them."

Mandy looked down and picked up the gold heart. Inscribed on it was the word FOREVER. Next to it on the gold chain was Logan's class ring.

"Oh, Logan, it's beautiful! Thank you."

"Now you're officially my girl." He started singing the words to the song "My Girl." Mandy giggled. Logan once more swept her hair away from her neck. This time he kissed her neck and moved around to her mouth. His kiss took her breath away. Logan's hands moved up and down her body. When his hand slipped under her blouse, Mandy sat up. She pushed his hand away.

"You need to stop, Logan."

"But you're my girl now. I know you care for me. I'm just trying to make you feel good. Weren't you enjoying it?"

Mandy couldn't lie. "Yes, but it's wrong."

"I love you, Mandy. I wouldn't do anything to hurt you."

Mandy was confused. She knew she loved Logan too.

Then one night Logan told Mandy, "I'll be leaving the end of July to go live with my dad in Pocatello, Idaho. He owns a thriving construction business and wants to make me a partner. I'd love for you to drive there with me to meet him.

I'll fly you home. I could show you around. The scenery is breathtaking with the magnificent northern Rocky Mountains, the towering Grand Tetons, and pine trees. There's great places to hike. And you should see the sky at night."

Mandy faced a dilemma. *Logan's leaving. I'm going away to college. But I love Logan.* She couldn't imagine a day without him.

———◦◦◦———

All summer long Allie noticed how enamored Mandy was with Logan. He was all she talked about. When she wasn't with him, they were on the phone together.

"Mandy, be careful. You have your whole life ahead of you. Don't forget about your career plans."

"Don't you get it, Mom? Logan's moving to Idaho with his dad at the end of the summer."

Allie breathed a sigh of relief. *This will give Mandy time to get him out of her system and back on track to pursue her education and get back into fellowship at church.*

"Mom, I love him. I can't imagine my life without him."

Allie felt as if someone had knocked all the wind out of her stomach, knowing that whatever she said, Mandy would just push back. Allie decided she needed to bring all this to the Lord. When Mandy went to bed that night, Allie sat at her desk with her Bible in her lap. Pulling her prayer journal off the shelf she opened it and wrote one word: HELP. Tears welled up as she read and wrote out Psalm 121:1-2. "I look to the hills. From whence comes my help. My help comes from the Lord who made heaven and earth."

≈ 15 ≈

Mandy never mentioned Logan's invitation for her to ride out to Idaho with him. After all it was more than an eleven-hour drive to Pocatello. Her mother would never agree to such a thing. The city did have a regional airport. It would be easy for her to fly home. The more Mandy thought about it, the more inviting the idea became. She always wanted to go on a road trip, and they would be mostly traveling through Utah, a state Mandy wanted to explore. This trip would be like a vacation before she started college in the fall.

Mandy was anxious to meet Logan's dad. For weeks Logan talked of nothing else. One day he said something to her while they were sitting in his car that took her by surprise. "One of the main reasons I wanted you to see Pocatello is because we'll probably live there after we're married. It's a great place to raise kids."

Mandy's head started spinning. *Did Logan say married?* Pictures of them standing at the altar danced in her head. *Oh my! He really does love me.* This time Mandy pulled Logan close, passionately kissing him.

"Wow, Mandy," Logan gasped, squirming under her, "What's got into you?"

"You, Logan Walker. I'm just loving you."

"Well, don't stop, babe."

Once again they almost crossed the line of no return. This

time it was Logan who stopped. "Hey, slow down. Not here. I want it to be perfect when it happens."

Mandy pulled away, discouraged.

———◦———

A week before Logan's departure he asked, "So your Mom's okay with you driving out with me?'

"I haven't told her."

"What?"

"Logan, you know she'll say no."

"Then just come. Call her when we're on the road. You're a big girl."

Mandy was torn between her promise never to defy her mother again and her desire to go to Idaho with Logan—a once-in-a-lifetime trip. She was sure she could keep Logan under control. He said they would drive straight through and not have to stop at a motel, only stop to eat and use the restroom. Logan planned on leaving at 4:00 a.m. This way they'd get an early start. Mandy made her decision.

"I'm going with you."

16

The easiest part was sneaking her suitcase out of the house a few days earlier. This morning she set her alarm for 4:00 a.m. She put together a tote bag and some snacks. Then she jotted a note to her mom:

Mom, I'm sorry. I drove to Idaho with Logan to meet his dad. I really wanted to see the countryside. He's flying me back home in a week. Please don't be angry. I love you, Mandy

Quietly she left the note on her mother's desk and slipped out of the house. The plan was for her to walk around the block to meet Logan. This way if her mother accidentally woke up she wouldn't find Mandy standing outside, and she'd think Mandy had already left. As soon as Mandy rounded the block, Logan pulled up. He handed her a Starbucks.

"How did you get this? They aren't open yet."

"I bought it last night and heated it up this morning. I know you love your latte."

"And I love you." She squeezed his knee and kissed him on the cheek.

They watched the sun rise as they traveled down the mountain. It was beautiful. Logan brought bagels that they ate for breakfast. Around 11:00 a.m. they stopped just outside Zion for lunch. They had traveled through mountains, high plateaus, and deserts. After a quick lunch of hamburgers and fries, they drove through Zion National Park, stopping often to take pictures together. Most of the tedious driving was over. They stopped in Salt Lake City for dinner. Logan ordered filet mignon and a baked potato for them. Allie shut her phone off when they left California. She noticed there were ten missed calls from her mother and several text messages. The feeling of guilt overwhelmed her. She kept pushing it out of her mind.

They arrived at Joe Walker's place at 6:00 p.m. Joe kind of reminded her of an old hippie. His hair was almost to his shoulders, and he wore a bandana around his forehead. "So this is the girl who made my son fall in love?"

Mandy blushed.

Joe went to the refrigerator and came back with some beers. He offered Mandy one. She refused. Logan gladly took one. Mandy excused herself since she wanted to freshen up. She beckoned to Logan.

"Where do I sleep?"

"Come, I'll show you. Be right back, Dad." Thankfully the house had three bedrooms. He led her upstairs to a small attic bedroom. It had a single bed and a small dresser. Next door to it was a bathroom with a shower.

"You can sleep here, Mandy. I'm taking the bedroom downstairs next to Dad. It has a king-size bed."

"Okay. I'm going to shower and change. See you soon."

Logan kissed her, turned and left.

The hot water felt good to Mandy as she showered. It took away the stiffness from the long ride in the car. Mandy threw on a pair of jeans and a Henley and went downstairs. Surprised she noticed lots of empty beer cans on the patio floor.

"Hey, there's my girl," shouted Logan. "Come over here."

Mandy walked over and Logan spun her around.

"Dad, did you ever see such a luscious woman?"

Before his dad could answer, Logan swooped her up and put her on his lap.

Mandy felt very uncomfortable with him manhandling her like that. *Is he showing off for his dad?*

"Come on, babe, snuggle up here with me." His breath reeked of beer. He disgusted her.

"No, Logan. I came down to say good night. I'm tired after the long drive."

"Okay." He pushed her off. Then he slapped her on her behind. "Get going then."

Startled, Mandy turned and left. She could hear Logan and his father laughing as she walked away.

The next few days Logan took Mandy on a tour of Pocatello. They saw very little of Joe. Logan said he was in the middle of a big construction job and had a girlfriend on the other side of town. Mandy didn't mind because all Logan's dad wanted was to drink beer with his son.

The first stop on their sightseeing adventure was the Museum of Clean. The museum had exhibits of historic cleaning techniques. Mandy was amazed to see the world's first vacuum. She wondered how a housewife maneuvered something like that. Their next stop was the Idaho Museum of Natural History. Mandy's favorite was the dinosaur exhibit. Logan enjoyed the walking tour of historic downtown Pocatello. They went into all the little shops to purchase fun treats. Mandy loved the unassuming mountain town, which she learned is known as the Gateway to the Northwest.

They finished their sightseeing day with an extensive hike followed by a refreshing dip into the hot-springs mineral pools.

≈17≈

Mandy's flight home was scheduled for Sunday. Thursday night Logan informed her that his dad needed to go to Salt Lake City for a few days to pick up some equipment. "I have a special surprise planned for you."

"What is it, Logan? Tell me. Please, tell me." She pleaded until he gave in.

"All right, Mandy. You win. I'm having a romantic dinner catered from the most famous restaurant in Pocatello for us tonight. Let's get dressed up."

Fortunately Mandy had packed a cute black spaghetti-strap dress. Wanting to look perfect Mandy spent extra time on her make-up and hair. She put her hair up in a rhinestone clip with tendrils hanging down. It made her look sophisticated. When Mandy came downstairs and walked into the dining room, Logan's eyes grew big and he whistled.

Mandy took one look at the display and her hand flew to her mouth, "Oh my, look at this! You really did plan a romantic dinner."

The table was covered with a white linen tablecloth with sparkling silver serving platters and white dinnerware with silver trim. There were even silver candlesticks. Logan removed the lids off the serving platter, displaying mounds of lasagna, ravioli, eggplant parmesan, and spaghetti. Italian desserts of cannoli and tiramisu complemented the meal.

Logan poured the wine and toasted. "To the girl of my dreams. My forever love."

Mandy's heart was about to burst. She drank more wine

than she should have, assuming with all the food she consumed the wine wouldn't have any effect on her. Feeling overly giddy, she realized she was hanging all over Logan. He didn't seem to mind. Logan just continued to affirm how beautiful she was and how much in love with her he was.

After they finished dessert he asked, "Why don't we jump in the pool? Work off some of these calories?"

"Sounds good. I'll go change into my suit."

As Mandy changed into her bathing suit, she realized she was a little tipsy. One thing was on her mind—Logan's kisses. She walked out on the pool deck and Logan whooped.

"There's my sexy lady."

Logan splashed water at her. She noticed Logan's swim trunks draped over the chair. He saw her look from the trunks to him. He laughed.

"Hey, Mandy, it feels real good to skinny dip. Why don't you try it? I'll turn around while you jump in. Look, I put towels right by the edge of the pool for when you're ready to come out. Promise not to look."

Mandy thought about it. Her inhibitions were dulled. "All right. But turn around."

Logan obeyed. Mandy slipped out of her two-piece suit and jumped in. Logan was right. She felt so free. She swam a few laps. Out of breath, she suddenly felt cold. Her body shook with chills.

Logan swam over to her. He pressed his body into hers. "Mandy, you're freezing. Let me get you a towel."

He hopped out of the pool. Mandy tried to look away. He held up a large towel and turned his head. Mandy climbed out of the pool. Logan wrapped the towel around her and picked her up.

"I turned on the gas fireplace in the living room before I got in the pool. It should be plenty warm in there now."

Gently he set Mandy down in front of the fireplace. Logan sat behind her wrapping his arms around her waist. "I love you so much, Mandy. You're my heart. I hope you enjoyed tonight."

"Oh yes, Logan, thank you! It was so very thoughtful of you."

Logan's lips found the back of Mandy's neck, then her shoulders, down her back. Slowly the towel fell from her shoulders. Logan supported her back. His kisses found their way to her front. The room spun. Mandy felt as though she were dropping fast on a Ferris wheel.

⟨≈ 18 ≈⟩

Mandy woke up to the sun on her face coming through a window. She looked around. It wasn't her room. She heard snoring and turned her head. In bed next to her lay Logan. *Oh no, I'm in his room. In his bed! God, what have I done?*

Mandy quietly slipped out of bed and ran up to her room. Grabbing some clothes she went into the bathroom and turned on the water. Getting on her knees in the shower she cried her heart out. "God, please, forgive me. What have I done? This is not how it should be."

She went back to her room, locked the door, and climbed into bed. She awoke to knocking at the door. "Mandy, open the door."

"Go away, Logan. I want to be alone."

"Okay, suit yourself. I'm running into town. Be back soon."

Mandy slept most of the day. When it was turning dark outside, Logan once more knocked on her door. "Please, Mandy, come on out. We need to talk."

After minutes of no response, he continued, "Anyway I know you must be hungry. I made a batch of blueberry pancakes. I know they're your favorite."

Mandy's stomach growled. Hunger took over. She opened the door.

"Let's go get something to eat." Logan took her by the hand.

Logan cooked the pancakes. Neither of them spoke much until after they finished eating.

"I'm sorry for what happened, Mandy. I guess my hormones took over. I just wanted you so bad."

"What we did was wrong. It's against everything I believe. It's something God says you save for the man you marry. What if I'm pregnant?"

"I understand. That's why we need to talk."

Logan took a small box out of his pocket. He placed it down in front of Mandy.

"What's this?"

"Open it."

Carefully Mandy lifted the lid of the blue velvet box. Inside she saw a beautiful pear-shaped diamond ring.

She gasped. Her eyes widened. She held her breath as her hand flew over her mouth.

"Marry me, Mandy. I love you and want to spend the rest of my life with you. And the pregnant thing, that would be taken care of since we'd be married."

Mandy stared at him. Words would not escape from her mouth.

"You could stay here and go to Idaho State University. I'd pay your first-semester tuition. In six months you'll be considered a resident. We could live here with my dad. With the money I'll be making, we'd be able to buy our own home within a year."

Mandy felt as if the room were spinning out of control and all the air was being sucked out of her. *Logan Walker wants to marry ME! Spend the rest of his life with me. Have children with me.* Mandy had often fantasized about this. Never in her wildest dreams could she imagine it becoming a reality.

Reason took over. "Logan, what about my mother, my home, and my college plans?"

"This will be your home now. I'll be your family. All I want, Mandy, is to love you and care for you for the rest of your life."

Removing the ring from the box, she slipped it on her finger. It fit perfectly. Mandy rationalized away her doubts. *Once we're married, of course, Logan and I will attend church together. Mom will give us her blessing. Or will she?* Images of the perfect Hallmark-movie marriage and family danced in Mandy's head. She succumbed to these images and let her reason be swept away by her romantic fantasy. Every young girl dreams of a cute little house surrounded by a white picket fence with children and dogs playing in the yard. At that very moment Mandy believed her dream was coming true. She flew into Logan's arms.

"Yes, yes, I'll marry you!"

≈ 19 ≈

Two weeks had gone by since Mandy left with Logan. At first Allie pursued her daughter with phone calls and text messages. She stopped when there was no response and gave it to God. Sitting down at her desk, she prayed for Mandy. She asked for protection for her daughter. She opened up her prayer journal and wrote down Isaiah 26:3:

> You will keep in perfect peace him whose mind is steadfast because he trusts in You.

I trust You, Lord, with my daughter. So I will be at peace. I will keep my mind on what You say, not on what I see.

Allie also jotted down Isaiah 49:25:

> For I will contend with him who contends with you. And I will save (defend, preserve, rescue, deliver) your children.

Allie ended her prayer time by thanking and praising God that he would bring Mandy home.

A few days later, Allie decided to give Elaine, Logan's mother, a call. She knew Elaine loved her son and probably was missing him too.

Elaine invited Allie to come over to her house. "Allie, we need to talk."

Elaine was very gracious and offered Allie coffee and some of her homemade strawberry-rhubarb pie.

"I invited you here because I know your daughter, Mandy, went with my son to Idaho. Believe me, I tried my hardest to talk him out of taking her. Unfortunately he's stubborn just like his dad, Joe. Joe and I were married right out of high school. I was starry-eyed over him. He was charismatic and handsome. The first years of our marriage were good. Joe's parents helped us out a lot financially. His dad set him up in his own construction business. I got a scholarship to nursing school. Once I became a registered nurse, I worked different shifts. Joe worked all day. When I worked on the night shift, he started going out with the boys after work. He started drinking. He used alcohol to self-medicate. His behavior became erratic. He became aggressive and couldn't control his anger. It got so I was afraid of him. One night, I started to feel sick at work, and they sent me home early. I caught him in our bed with another woman. I threatened to leave him. He swore up and down it would never happen again. I loved him and I stayed.

"Two months later I found out I was pregnant. I started having complications and was put on bed rest. Joe was supportive, but by the third month he grew restless. At first he went out for a few drinks after work with his co-workers. Next he would go out on weekends. He would come home drunk late at night. Several times I smelled perfume on his clothes. When Logan was born, he stayed home more and drank at home. One night I suggested he get help. 'You have a drinking problem,' I told him.

"As soon as I said those words, he went berserk. I took Logan and left. I could no longer live with an alcoholic. So I divorced Joe.

"Throughout the years he paid child support and shared custody. Logan wanted to go live with his dad when he was twelve years old. By that time I was married to Henry. He was the exact opposite of Joe. I couldn't have asked for a more unselfish loving man. He loved Logan like a father should. I fought against Logan going to live with his dad, but Henry said Logan needed this. I feared he would learn bad habits from Joe—drinking and womanizing.

"Logan returned to live with us after he and his dad got into a fight. Joe is selfish and demanding, and Logan just couldn't deal with it. Now Joe wants him back. He baited him by promising him a partnership in his construction business. Henry and I wanted Logan to go to college and stay here. He certainly had the grades for it. I was happy when Logan started dating Mandy. She's such a good girl. She got him to go to church with her. Allie, I love my son, but I'm afraid he's too much like his dad. I don't want Mandy to get hurt."

"Thank you for the information. Would you pray with me for our children?"

"Of course."

Allie took Elaine's hands in hers. She bowed her head and prayed, "Lord, You said if two or more agree together in Your name, You are in the midst of them. We ask for protection over our children. Give them wisdom in the decisions they make."

Elaine continued. "Lord, bring our children home."

Elaine promised Allie to stay in touch and share any contact she had with Logan.

⇒20⇐

Mandy persuaded Logan to promise no more intimacy until they were married. She continued to sleep in a separate room. Logan's dad returned home and wasn't excited about their news.

"You're a sweet girl, Mandy, but my son isn't ready for marriage."

Pulling Logan aside he said, "Your mom and I got married young and look at where that ended up. Besides, Logan, this is the time in your life you should be having fun and dating lots of girls."

"Mandy and I are not Mom and you. Mandy is all I need right now."

"We'll see," Joe said, shaking his head and walking away.

Although Mandy felt like she was totally happy, at the same time she was ridden with guilt. *My Mom—I know I've hurt her deeply. I just abandoned her.* Several times Mandy sat down to write a letter to Allie. She couldn't find the right words. She knew her mom would be disappointed in her. Deep in her heart she knew she was wrong. She just couldn't make herself leave Logan.

Mandy started school at Idaho State University. Logan began working construction. He wasn't used to manual labor. Every night, he came home exhausted, complaining about how hard he worked. Usually he drank a beer and fell asleep on the couch.

Mandy loved college. She spent countless hours studying. During the week Logan and Mandy rarely saw one another since Mandy stayed after hours at the school library. By the time she arrived home, Logan was passed out. On weekends Mandy studied. Logan slept a lot or sat around drinking beer with his dad. He showed no interest in Mandy's college courses nor how she was doing in school.

Mandy questioned Logan about a wedding date. He brushed her off saying, "Let me save some more money for a proper wedding."

When she petitioned him again months later, he responded, "I'm saving money for our honeymoon."

The more Mandy prodded him, the more frustrated he became. "It's going to happen, Mandy. Just don't push me."

What Logan failed to understand was she wanted the marriage to happen more for the restoration of the relationship between her and her mother.

Time seemed to pass quickly. Christmas came and went. Mandy longed for her mother and home. Logan and his dad's idea of Christmas was lots of food and drinking and going to a pool hall. All they gloated about was that they had time off.

Christmas in Big Bear was magical. Her mother made every Christmas memorable. Disgusted, Mandy left for most of Christmas day to accompany her friend Jennifer from school to help out at a homeless shelter. She left the center feeling like she at least helped the homeless children have a merry Christmas. She arrived home in the evening only to find Logan and Joe passed out, leaving a huge mess in the kitchen.

Mandy maintained a 4.0 grade-point average, and her professors loved her. She attended classes three days a week. The other days she worked at the school library. Eventually she spent more time at school than at Logan's dad's house. Logan never complimented her or told her how proud he was of her efforts. He merely complained about his work or about her not doing his laundry or cleaning the house.

"You get to sit in a nice air-conditioned building, while I'm out breaking my back in extreme weather."

"Logan, I'm working towards getting a degree to help our family financially."

"Whatever." Logan threw up his hands and went into the kitchen to grab another beer.

≈ 21 ≈

Things weren't always bad. Some Saturdays Logan would take her on a picnic or on a hike. He never brought up the wedding again. Mandy didn't want to get him angry. So she decided to let it go. *Surely we'll have enough money by the summer to get married.* Mandy tried to convince herself.

Summer came and went. Then another depressing holiday season. Mandy ached for her mother. *I can't go home unmarried. What will Mom think of me? I can't shame her.*

Mandy and Logan grew farther apart. The longer she lived at Joe's house, the more she saw Logan was just like his dad. Logan never again mentioned them getting married. Mandy just focused on school. She planned to take classes throughout the summer to complete her degree sooner. Right before summer school was to begin, Mandy had two weeks off. She and Jennifer had decided to do some fun things together. Jennifer also worked at the library with Mandy and became the friend she confided in.

One night Mandy came home from school and found Logan sitting at the kitchen table. Surprisingly he hadn't been drinking.

"Hey, Mandy, I know we've kind of drifted apart. Different schedules. Different lives. I've missed you. Listen, today my cousin Bryan, who lives about three hours away, contacted me. His company is celebrating being in business for twenty-five years. They're holding a three-day party at

Bear Lake State Park. It's a beautiful place with turquoise blue water. You can camp, waterski, fish, and swim. Bryan's bringing his boat. It should be lots of fun. One of the guys from work said I could borrow his RV. What do you say?"

Mandy thought about it. *Maybe this is just what we need to re-connect and get back on track to be married.* "Sure, it sounds like a good time. It's perfect timing. I'm off now and still have another week until the summer session begins."

———— • ————

Mandy went shopping with Jennifer right before she left on her adventure with Logan. She wanted to pick out some cute new clothes. They stopped to get some coffee.

Jennifer looked concerned. "Mandy, I know we haven't been friends that long, but I'm worried about you. You've been with this guy for almost two years. You're wearing his engagement ring. Yet you tell me he avoids setting a wedding date. I think you deserve better."

Mandy made excuses for Logan. "I appreciate your concern. Logan just started working in his dad's construction business, and I'm super busy with school. It'll happen."

"How long are you going to keep your life on hold for him? What about your mom? Every time you talk about her there's so much sadness in your eyes."

Mandy sighed. "I know. This long weekend will be the perfect time to bring up the wedding. I've been thinking a December wedding would be perfect with Christmas decorations and all."

"All right, Mandy, I'll pray for wisdom and clarity for you."

"Thanks, Jennifer."

⚬22⚬

On the drive out to Bear Lake State Park, Logan seemed like his old self. He was attentive and affectionate towards her. *This is totally what we needed,* thought Mandy.

The first day was amazing. Bryan's sailboat was so much fun. His girlfriend, Robin, seemed nice, although Mandy thought Robin's clothing was a bit too revealing. She and Bryan were all over one another. It made Mandy uncomfortable.

After the boat ride they swam, barbecued, and built a fire on the beach. Things began to change. Bryan brought out some liquor when several other couples joined them. Everyone was drinking and getting pretty wild. The language and their jokes offended Mandy. She grew tired and started to get a headache. She excused herself, went back to the RV, and fell right to sleep.

She was abruptly awakened by Logan stumbling in and knocking a glass off the table. He fell into bed next to her. She feigned sleep. He reeked of alcohol.

———

The next morning she woke to the smell of coffee. She passed Logan on the way to the shower.

"Sorry, babe. I guess I drank too much. Why did you leave so early?"

Mandy's eyes narrowed. "I don't enjoy sitting around watching people get drunk and obnoxious."

Logan sighed and shrugged his shoulders.

Mandy came out of the shower to find Logan had cooked bacon and eggs. "Thanks for breakfast."

"We're going fishing today. One of Bryan's co-workers has a large fishing boat. We were invited along with eight other couples. He's supplying lunch."

"I love fishing. Remember how you used to take me out in your stepfather's pontoon boat on Big Bear Lake? It's pretty funny. We'll be fishing on Big Bear Lake here in Idaho too."

"You're going to love the fishing boat. We'll probably catch a whole lot more than we did in California. This lake is loaded with fish."

———※———

Mandy did enjoy fishing. She caught four rainbow trout. Logan caught two mountain whitefish and four cutthroat trout. They laughed together all day, especially when the first fish Mandy caught slipped off the hook and flopped around the boat. She caught it and it jumped out of her hand.

Bryan told Logan, "We're putting all the fish on ice, and tomorrow we're having a huge fish fry. Tonight everyone wants to go to Garden City. They're known for one of the best steakhouses in the state. Right next door there's a saloon that has line-dancing with instructors to help you learn the steps."

The Stagecoach Inn had the most delicious steak Mandy ever ate. The restaurant had buckets of peanuts on the tables, and you threw the shells on the floor.

After dinner they walked over to the saloon where a live country band was playing. Bryan was right. The instructors taught them the Texas two-step. Mandy caught on quickly, and they danced until the place closed at 2:00 a.m.

Mandy was glad Logan wasn't driving. Once again he

had too much beer to drink. *Why can't he just have fun without drinking?* They both fell asleep on the way home. Back at the RV they were beyond tired and crashed in their clothes.

23

When they woke up Logan told her, "Bryan and Robin invited us over this morning for a pancake breakfast."

"Okay. I'll take a quick shower. Be ready in a few minutes."

When they arrived Bryan was setting up the griddle outside. Robin was in the kitchen squeezing oranges to make fresh orange juice. Logan went outside to help Bryan and set up the picnic table. Mandy gathered the maple syrup and butter to bring outside.

Robin looked intently at Mandy. "So what's your story?"

"What do you mean?"

"Well, you're wearing an engagement ring. Bryan asked Logan the other night if you guys were planning on getting married. He said, 'Not anytime soon.' Listen, Bryan and I have lived together for five years. We like it that way. No contract. No strings. Neither of us feels tied down. We still enjoy being together. We think marriage ruins a relationship."

"I'm sorry, Robin, I don't agree with you. When two people love one another, there needs to be a commitment. God intended it that way."

"God? Oh, so you're one of those religious people. I understand now. That's why you wouldn't drink with us. 'Holier than thou.' I really don't think Logan's down with all that Jesus stuff."

"Maybe not right now."

"So you think you're going to change your man?"

"Yes, I do."

"Sorry, sister. It'll never happen. Men don't change."

———◦———

Just then Logan walked in. "Pancakes are ready." Taking one look at Mandy's face, he knew something was wrong. He slipped his arm around her waist. "Hey, are you okay, sweetheart?"

Robin rolled her eyes.

"Fine," Mandy mumbled.

During breakfast the guys chatted about the fish fry. Robin said she made a big pot of cheese grits. Mandy told her she made some macaroni salad to bring.

"There should be plenty of food and beer. Let's clean up. I want to take the sailboat out today. We just might catch the sunset tonight," announced Bryan.

———◦———

It was a perfect day on the lake. Mandy tried to push her conversation with Robin out of her mind. What does she know anyway? She lay back in the seat, letting the motion of the boat relax her, determined nothing would spoil their last day at the lake.

After an hour or so, Logan asked Bryan, "You got anything to drink?"

"So glad you asked." Bryan retuned with a cooler full of beer and wine coolers.

"Here, Mandy." Bryan handed her a wine cooler.

"No thanks. I'll just have water."

Bryan and Logan exchanged looks. Mandy noticed a scowl on Logan's face. Logan said very little to her the rest of the boat ride. He just continued to drink.

=24=

The fish fry was all set up and ready when they returned to shore. Mandy ate until she thought she would burst. Then she sat down on the blanket Logan set out by the fire. She moved closer to him. His body grew stiff.

"What's wrong?"

"Why do you embarrass me all the time?"

"What do you mean?"

"Always acting like a church girl. Why don't you loosen up and have some fun?"

Mandy lay down and closed her eyes, almost falling asleep. Logan continued to drink and get loud. Somebody made a snide comment to him. He shouted, "We'll see about that."

The next thing she knew, Logan picked her up. He flung her over his shoulder. "You're my lady. You belong to me."

"Put me down. Put me down!"

He took her into the RV and threw her down on the bed. He forced himself on her. She screamed, scratched, and kicked. He put his hand over her mouth. He took what he wanted. When it was over he pounded his chest and went back outside.

She heard him howl. Mandy assumed he was announcing his conquest. She cried herself to sleep. *I can't do this anymore. He's an animal. Jennifer was right. He doesn't honor me. I have to get away from him. Oh, God, why did I ever come to*

Idaho with him? Why did I ever let him talk me into staying here? What if I'm pregnant?

Not a word was spoken between Mandy and Logan on the drive home. Logan drank coffee and ate donuts. Mandy munched on a granola bar and drank water. They found Joe drinking beer and watching television when they arrived home.

"You kids have fun?"

"Fishing was great," Logan answered. "And Bryan took us out in his sailboat."

Mandy kept her head down. Joe looked from Mandy to Logan. He shook his head. "I'm going to shoot some pool. Logan, want to come? It looks like you could use some time with your old man."

"Sure, Dad."

Without a word to Mandy, Logan left.

———◦◦◦———

As soon as she was certain they were gone, she called Jennifer and briefly shared the details of the weekend.

"I'm coming over," Jennifer announced. "You're not staying there. I don't want you spending another minute with Logan. He doesn't deserve you."

"Okay. I'll get my things together."

After gathering her belongings Mandy packed them in the old Volkswagen Joe had given her. It was in her name. So Mandy knew she could eventually sell it.

She took the ring off her finger and laid it on Logan's bed, along with the necklace and his class ring.

When Jennifer showed up Mandy followed her to her apartment. Jennifer helped her carry her things in.

"Sit down, Mandy. I'm making us some tea. I made some peanut butter cookies today. I know you like them. Help yourself."

Jennifer listened intently as Mandy shared the weekend events with her. By the end of the conversation, Mandy was sobbing. "I'm such a fool. I should have known he had no intention of marrying me."

"Mandy, I know your heart is broken now. I know someone who can put all the broken pieces of your life back together."

"Jesus?"

"Yes, that's right. You need to trust him to help you move on and get your life back. Start by coming to church with me."

Mandy felt so grateful to have a friend like Jennifer. They had a few days until classes began again. The girls slept in late, watched old movies, and ate popcorn and cookies. Every evening before bed, Jennifer would have a little Bible study for them. Mandy was surprised. She didn't even think about Logan.

Several times Logan called Mandy, begging her to come home. Mandy declined to answer. She sent him one text message: "My home is with my mother in California. Logan, I'm done with your lies and deceit." Then she blocked him on her phone.

$\Longrightarrow$ 25 $\Longrightarrow$

School started again. It felt good to Mandy to be back in class. She and Jennifer had two of the same classes. They often studied together. Jennifer didn't charge Mandy any rent. Her last roommate had transferred schools. The former roommate's parents paid the rest of the year's rent. They told Jennifer to just keep the money.

Mandy attended church with Jennifer. She liked the pastor. His messages always seemed to be aimed right at her heart. She knew by now she needed to return home. Two things kept her from doing that right now. First, her period was late. She kept putting off seeing a doctor. Second, she had only four classes to finish her two-year degree. She signed up for the fall semester to complete these classes. Mandy's classes went well, and she continued to maintain her 4.0 grade point average.

One morning Jennifer approached Mandy. "Listen, I made an appointment for you with my doctor next month. You can't run away from this."

"You're right. Thanks for caring."

The day before the doctor appointment, Mandy rushed out of the bathroom. "Cancel the doctor appointment. I'm not pregnant. Thank You, Jesus!"

Sunday, October 8, their church planned a fall festival after the service. Jennifer and Mandy baked both a pumpkin and apple pie. Mandy would always remember this date and this Sunday. It was the day God gave her clear direction. The pastor preached a sermon from Luke 15. He titled his sermon "The Forgiving Father." The main message was that it does not matter how far we stray away from our heavenly Father or how much we squander the gifts He provides. He is always delighted when we turn back to Him. His unconditional love is waiting for us to return home where He greets us with open arms.

She told Jennifer after church, "That message was God telling me what to do."

"Huh?"

"I know God has forgiven me. He's the forgiving Father. When Pastor Fred talked about Him wanting us to return home, I saw my mother. I know she'll greet me with open arms. She's already forgiven me. As soon as classes are done, I'm heading home."

"I'm so happy for you, Mandy. You have to promise to stay in touch."

"Of course. You rescued me. You're a very special friend."

Jennifer's parents came to visit the girls for Thanksgiving. Her mom cooked a feast. Mandy loved them, and they loved her. She saw now why Jennifer was such a caring person.

The day Jennifer's parents left to go back home, Jennifer's dad handed Mandy an envelope. "We won't see you at Christmas. Here's a little something for you when you get home." On the front of the envelope were the words: "Don't open until Christmas."

She thanked and hugged them both.

Mandy's finals were over on December 15. She sold the Volkswagen to one of the girls in her class. She used some of the money to purchase an airline ticket home. She planned on leaving on December 16. Jennifer drove her to the airport. They both cried. At almost the same time both girls pulled out a box and handed it to the other. Laughing they said in unison, "Merry Christmas." More hugs.

Mandy boarded the plane. She decided to save Jennifer's present, along with her dad's gift, until Christmas.

Mandy arrived at Ontario airport around 5:00 p.m. She had booked a room at a motel, not wanting to drive up the mountain in the dark.

The next morning she rented a car that she could return in Big Bear Lake. Mandy stopped at the mall. She wanted to buy some Christmas gifts for her mom. She found a forest green sweater, her mom's favorite color. Next she bought a bottle of Chanel perfume—the fragrance that her mother wore. Walking back to the car, she noticed a stand selling candied pecans. *Mom loves these.* She bought a gift box of pecans. She stopped to get a latte and a bagel. After her breakfast she started on her journey home. Mandy sang praise songs and thanked God that He led her back home.

⟞ 26 ⟝

Allie just finished cleaning up the kitchen after having dinner. She went into the living room and sat down at her desk. She opened her Bible to Jeremiah 31:16-17. In her prayer journal she wrote:

> *Restrain your voice from weeping and your eyes from tears, for your work will be rewarded, declares the Lord. They will return from the land of the enemy.*

Father, You never give up on Your children. Neither will I give up on my daughter, Mandy.

She closed her Bible. Getting up, she thought she heard a car outside.

When Mandy walked up the steps, a porch light flicked on. Mandy gasped. The Christmas sign! She read it slowly. "All hearts come home for Christmas. Welcome home." She smiled, remembering the day she and her mom bought the sign. God knew one day that sign would mean everything to them.

From where Allie stood she thought she saw someone pass by the front window. She jumped when the doorbell rang. *Now who could that be?* Allie opened the door. Her mouth fell open and her eyes grew wide. She stood unmoving.

Mandy fell into her arms. Words weren't necessary as mother and daughter embraced one another. Allie spoke first. "Thank You, Jesus. I knew I could trust You to bring her home."

Bear ran up and licked Mandy's face.

"Hi, Bear. Good dog." She squatted down and hugged the dog. "I missed you too."

Allie thought her heart would burst. "I know what we need. Some Christmas tea. I'll go make some." She retreated to the kitchen.

Mandy glanced around the room. *Nothing's changed. I'm home and home to stay.*

In its faithful place in the corner of the living room by the window stood a freshly cut Frasier fir tree. Mandy stepped closer, touching each ornament. Memories flooded her mind. Tears rolled down her cheeks.

Allie came back in. "I've got us a treat to go with the tea."

Mandy turned around slowly, wiping the tears from her face.

"Pumpkin scones."

"Yummy, Mom. You know I can't resist them."

Allie chatted on about her sister, Amy, and her husband, Ben. She told Mandy about their church. "Our youth pastor is leaving to pastor his own church. Pastor Tom's brother's son just finished Bible college. He's coming to be the new youth pastor. He'll be introduced at church tomorrow."

Mandy didn't say much. She just stared at her mom. She notice some new frown lines on Allie's forehead and some around her eyes. *Those are probably my doing.* What she noticed the most was how Allie's face glowed. Her mother hadn't stopped smiling since Mandy appeared at the front door.

Allie glanced at the clock. "It's getting late. Church is tomorrow. We have the rest of our lives to catch up."

"Right, Mom. I'm tired too. I'm going to bed. I love you. See you in the morning."

"Love you too." Allie hugged her daughter.

⚞ 27 ⚟

Allie awoke the next morning with Mandy and Bear sitting on the side of her bed. "Is it that time already?"

"Yes, Mom. Bear slept with me. He licked my face when he wanted to go out. I took him for a walk. I've already taken a shower. Why don't you shower while I make us some breakfast?"

"Sounds like a plan." Allie sat up and hugged her daughter. "So good to have you home."

Mandy smiled. "It's good to be home."

Allie hadn't mentioned Logan, Idaho, or any of it. She figured if her daughter wanted to share anything with her she would. *All that's in the past. That's where it should stay—in the past.* Mandy made scrambled eggs, bacon, and toast. Allie shared a daily devotion.

———————

After breakfast they headed to the church. Mandy was greeted with open arms by the members of the congregation. Pastor Tom personally came up to her. "Welcome home, Mandy. It's so great to have you home. We've missed your smiling face."

"Thank you, Pastor Tom. It's great to be home. I've missed you and the church too. You're like family." She noticed a tall, handsome young man standing behind the pastor.

"Oh, Mandy, this is my nephew Joshua," the pastor said. "He's going to be our new youth pastor."

Joshua extended his hand, "Pleasure to meet you, Mandy."

She almost jumped. A jolt of electricity went down her arm when he shook her hand.

When Pastor Tom introduced Joshua to the church, Mandy noticed he smiled and looked right at her. He had the kindest eyes she'd ever seen.

———◦———

After church Allie followed Mandy to drop off the rental car. They stopped at the grocery store to pick up a few things for dinner. When they got home they added the vegetables to the crock pot. Mandy made a salad.

At dinner Mandy shared with her mom. "I completed my associate degree at Idaho State University. I maintained a 4.0 grade point average. Before I left I checked into California Baptist University in Riverside. They accepted all my credits, so I enrolled. I start classes there in January to finish my bachelor's degree in social work."

"That's great. I'm so proud of you. Liz from church mentioned to me this morning that the Department of Family and Children's Services is looking for a part-time receptionist. Maybe that could work out for you while you're attending school."

———◦———

The next few days Mandy randomly ran into Joshua. She went to the post office. He was there. She stopped to get gas. She found him pumping gas too. Even at the grocery store he was in the line next to her.

One day she stopped at Starbucks. Walking in she heard someone say, "Are you stalking me?"

She looked over her shoulder. There was Joshua.

"What are you doing here?" she asked.

"Drinking coffee and reading a book. Would you like to sit down?"

"Okay, for a minute. I have to go order my drink first."

"What are you having? I'll go get it."

"Thanks. A decaf non-fat latte. Grande size."

She picked up the book Joshua was reading. *A Christmas Carol*. He returned, handed her the drink, and sat down.

"Thanks. Do you always read classics?"

"I like to read *A Christmas Carol* every Christmas. It puts me in the spirit. Why, do you like to read the classics?"

"Yes. My favorite is *Wuthering Heights* by Emily Bronte."

"The love story of Heathcliff and Cathy."

"You read it too?"

"Of course. A tragic love story. I think Emily Bronte's suffering and death at thirty was just as tragic."

Mandy was impressed that Joshua knew so much about literature. "I need to go and get these groceries home to my mom. Thanks again for the drink."

"No problem. Maybe we can discuss the classics again."

He smiled at Mandy. She noticed his chocolate-colored eyes perfectly matched his auburn hair. A lock of his hair had fallen over one of his eyes. She had a sudden impulse to brush it away. She restrained herself, turned around, waved, and left.

⟨ 28 ⟩

On Christmas Eve Mandy and Allie attended a musical at church. A potluck was to follow the performance. They had baked pumpkin, apple, and pecan pies to bring. The musical was called "Rejoice with the Angels." The message was the story of Christ's birth told by an angel. It contrasted what happened on earth with what happened in heaven during that blessed event. The play inspired the audience to think about what actually was happening in heaven the night Jesus was born on earth. The finale was amazing. Joshua sang a solo of "O Holy Night." The congregation was awestruck. He received a standing ovation. *This guy is just too much. What other surprises does he have?*

After the program, Allie and her mom filled their plates, found a table, and sat down.

"Mom, where did Joshua come from?"

"He lived in Nebraska."

Just then Joshua came over.

"Joshua, you have such a beautiful voice. You sound just like Andrea Bocelli," Allie commented.

"Thank you, Mrs. Morrison. You're very kind. I don't think I'm that good."

"Yes, you are," Mandy blurted out.

Joshua raised an eyebrow. "Why, thank you, Mandy." He winked and smiled at her.

Mandy blushed.

Joshua leaned over. "Would you like to go to dinner with me some time?"

"Maybe."

"Well, that's better than a no." He laughed. "I've been thinking I'd like to find someone to show me around Big Bear. I thought if you were willing to do that, I'd treat you to a nice dinner."

"We'll see."

Mandy and Allie spent Christmas Day at home together. Allie cooked a turkey. She layered some cooked stuffing around the turkey so that it would crisp up in the oven. Mandy made candied yams and layered some slices of cranberry, creating a colorful display. She also made a string-bean casserole. They still had two pies left from those they baked for the potluck.

Mandy opened the present from Jennifer. It was exactly the same present she had given to Jennifer. A heart charm inscribed with the words: "Friends Forever." Jennifer's dad had given Mandy two-hundred dollars with a card that read: "To a sweet young lady. Here's a little something to help with your college supplies."

Allie brought out old picture albums. They talked endlessly about the memories they shared.

When Allie made a pot of coffee to go with the dessert, Mandy announced, "It's time."

"Time for what?"

"Time to watch *It's a Wonderful Life*. It's our tradition."

"Okay. But instead of popcorn we'll eat the pie."

Before they sat down to watch the movie, Allie said, "Joshua's very nice. I think he's interested in getting to know you better."

"Yeah, Mom. He asked me to show him around Big Bear. He offered to take me out to dinner if I did."

"What did you say?"

"I told him I'd think about it."

"I think you should. He would be a good friend to have."

"You might be right, Mom. I'll tell him I'll do it."

As mother and daughter cuddled during the movie and enjoyed their dessert, Mandy glanced out the window. "Look, Mom. It's snowing."

"The snow's coming down in big heavy flakes now," Allie observed. "Oh wow, the temperature dropped. I'm going to get some more firewood to put in the wood stove."

"I'll help you. It looks like we're going to need a lot tonight."

After they brought in the wood, Mandy looked from the Christmas tree to her mom. "I'm glad you put up the tree again."

"I put a tree up every year since you left. I knew you loved our decorated Christmas tree. I wanted to have a tree up when you came home."

"Mom, this is the best Christmas ever because I'm home with you. I love you so much."

"And I love you, sweetie."

Mandy felt warm all over. It wasn't just the heat from the wood stove. It was the warmth of the love in her home.

29

Allie woke Mandy early the next morning.

"Mandy, Mandy, wake up! Come look outside."

"What, Mom?"

Mandy hurried downstairs. She found Allie at the front window. Everything outside was white, beautifully covered with fresh snow.

"It's got to be at least one to two feet," said Mandy.

They heard the sound of the snowplow coming down the street. Allie's driveway now had a berm in front of it.

A few hours later, Mandy and her mom sat drinking hot cocoa and eating cookies. There was a loud knock at the door. Allie got up to answer.

"Hi, Joshua. Come on in."

"Thank you, ma'am." He pulled off his snow boots.

"Sit down. I'll get you some hot cocoa. I have a fresh batch of peanut butter cookies coming out of the oven."

Joshua sat down across from Mandy. "Hi. How was your Christmas?"

"Wonderful. What about yours?"

"It was great. I ate too much, though. Aunt Joyce is a great cook."

Allie walked back in with cocoa and cookies.

"These are really good, Mrs. Morrison." Joshua said after his first bite. "My uncle sent me here with his snow blower to see if you needed someone to clear away your snow."

"That's really nice of your uncle to think of us."

Joshua spent a whole two hours blowing the snow off the

driveway, cleaning the snow off the porch, and shoveling away the berm. When Allie saw him working on the porch, she called out to him, "Come on in when you finish and warm yourself. I made a big pot of corn chowder and some corn bread."

"Thanks."

Joshua's face was beet red when he walked in. He took off his gloves, coat, boots, and soaking wet ski cap. Then he walked over to the wood stove. "This feels great."

Mandy set the table. She poured a mug of cocoa and handed it to Joshua. "This should warm you up."

He smiled at her.

Allie walked in from the kitchen carrying a soup tureen. "Soup's ready."

The three of them sat down. Allie asked Joshua to bless the food. His sincere blessing touched Mandy's heart.

"Mrs. Morrison, that's a really cool Christmas sign you have hanging outside on the porch."

"Mandy and I found it several Christmases ago. I bought it and told her I would hang it there so when she went away to college, she'd always know she was welcome home."

"Yes, and that's just what it did. When I came back from Idaho, it was the first thing I saw. I knew I was welcome. It's very special to me and Mom."

After they finished eating, Joshua looked over at Mandy. "So are you going to show me around Big Bear?"

"Yes, when the snow melts some."

"It's supposed to warm up by Saturday."

"All right. Let's plan on Saturday."

———⊷✦⊶———

The weather warmed up a little by the weekend, and the roads were cleared. Joshua picked Mandy up at 11:00 a.m.

The first place she took him was Snow Summit Ski Slope. They rode up the mountain on the ski lift. Joshua had grabbed a wool blanket out of the car when they arrived. He placed it over her as they rode.

They discovered a small restaurant at the top. They ordered tomato soup, grilled cheese, and hot cocoa. The view of the mountain and lake from the summit was beautiful.

Their next stop was Big Bear Alpine Zoo. Joshua liked the black bears the best. So did Mandy. After the zoo they drove to the Discovery Center. The center was featuring an exhibit on the wildlife of Big Bear.

Mandy suggested they walk around the village next. The temperature had warmed up by then, and the sun was shining brightly. Joshua enjoyed the tourist shops. He slipped into one without Mandy and came out with a stuffed black bear for her.

"Thanks. How did you know I liked bears?"

"I just knew."

They finished off their day with dinner at The Pines at Lakefront. The restaurant not only had a cabin decor but also an awesome view of the lake.

They shared the surf-and-turf dinner. Mandy ate the lobster while Joshua ate the steak. Joshua made Mandy feel comfortable. He was easy to talk to and showed a genuine interest in what she had to say.

When they got to her house he said, "I'd like to see you again."

"I'd like that too."

"When we were in the village I noticed the little theater was having a double-feature matinee this week. They're showing 'White Christmas' and 'Christmas in Connecticut.' Would you want to go tomorrow?"

"Sure! Those are two of my favorite old movies."

"Great. I'll pick you up at 11:00 o'clock. We'll go for coffee first."

"Bye. Thanks for the dinner."

⪻ 30 ⪼

Mandy and Joshua continued seeing one another. Both Pastor Tom and Allie were happy for the relationship. After dating Mandy for a little over seven months and much prayer, Joshua decided she was the one. He talked it over with Pastor Tom.

"Mandy's a sweet girl," the pastor said. "I've known her since she was a baby. She has a heart for Jesus. You need to be aware that she was deeply hurt by a man. God is still mending the broken pieces of her life. She's delicate. Be gentle with her. You have my blessing."

Mandy attended California Baptist University on Tuesdays and Thursdays. The other weekdays she worked at the Department of Family and Children Services.

One day the next spring, while Mandy was at school, Joshua visited Allie. "I'd like to ask your daughter to be my wife. I'm asking for your blessing."

Allie's hands flew to her chest. She ran over and hugged Joshua. "I would be honored to have you as a son-in-law. Actually you'd be my son-in-love. You two are good together. You're an answer to prayer. I've prayed for a godly husband for my daughter. I think Mandy will be a real asset to the youth ministry."

"Thank you. I agree she does great work with the kids."

They continued dating throughout the summer. July 31 was Joshua's birthday. Mandy planned a special day for him.

Little did she know it would turn out to be a special day for her as well.

In the morning they went for a hike on the Pine Knot Trail, which leads to Grand View Point where there were great lake and mountain views.

After the hike they both went back home to shower and get dressed for dinner. She picked him up at 4:30 p.m. Mandy had on a turquoise summer dress, and Joshua wore a turquoise shirt with khaki pants. They giggled when he got into the car and noticed their matching colors.

"Where are you taking me?"

"Just wait and see."

Mandy pulled the car into the parking lot of the Sweet Basil Bistro. It was a quaint little restaurant that served fresh country Italian cuisine. The waiter took them to a small table at the rear.

"Wow, this is romantic," Joshua observed.

"Yes. I like the intimate atmosphere."

There were white linen tablecloths on the tables along with candle lanterns with soft ambient light. Mandy handed Joshua a little box. "Happy birthday."

Inside was a 14K gold cross necklace. "Thanks. I love this. Here, put it on me."

"Okay. It looks great."

Joshua leaned over and squeezed her hand. Mandy ordered cheese ravioli and an antipasto salad. Joshua had the same salad and lobster lasagna. When Mandy made the dinner reservation, she ordered a tiramisu cake for Joshua's birthday. The waiter brought it out with five candles on it. The staff sang happy birthday to Joshua. The waiter told them he would cut two pieces and box up the rest for them to take home.

Joshua excused himself and walked towards the restroom.

The waiter set Mandy's piece of cake in front of her. She noticed something reflecting off the light of the lantern on the cake. Looking closer she discovered a ring lying on top of the cake. She glanced over at Joshua. He wasn't in his seat. Instead she found him kneeling on one knee by her side. Mandy's mouth flew open.

"Marry me," he said, his dark eyes fixed on hers.

Mandy could scarcely speak. Finally, when the words came out, she said, "We need to talk."

He rose and took her hand. "I love you, and I want to spend the rest of my life with you."

Mandy took a deep breath. "I love you too. But…"

"But what?"

"Let's finish our desserts and go somewhere to talk."

They finishing eating the cake without a word. Mandy paid the bill. Joshua pulled out her chair, took her hand, and led her to the car.

Mandy started her car. "I'm going to drive over to the park. We can talk there."

"Okay."

<hr>

They arrived at Boulder Bay Park. She parked the car, and they walked over to a table and sat down on the bench.

"So what's going on, Mandy?"

"I don't deserve you. You're too good for me. You need someone who's better for you. Someone who can be a pastor's wife. Someone who's pure. I ran away after high school with my boyfriend. Things happened that I'm ashamed of. I should have known better."

"Mandy, we've all made mistakes. One day I was tired of being a goody-goody preacher's kid. I rebelled against my parents. They still loved me and prayed for me. I drank, tried drugs, and partied until one of my closest friends got into a wreck. He was drinking and driving. He killed himself and his girlfriend. Both family's lives were ruined.

"This was my wake-up call. I repented, asked my parents for forgiveness, and gave my life totally to Christ. God forgave me, and He forgave you. When He died on the cross, He took all of our sins on Himself: past, present, and future. In the book of Hebrews Jesus says that He will forgive our wickedness and remember our sins no more. If He forgave you, Mandy, you need to forgive yourself. You also need to forgive the person who hurt you. That person is no longer tied to your destiny. You need to see yourself as God sees you—you're a daughter of the King. The apple of His eye. You need to trust God. He knows what you need, and He has a plan and a purpose for your life. He wants you to know Jesus' righteousness is what the Father sees when He looks at you. God loves you with an everlasting love."

Mandy started to cry. *Joshua is right. I've carried this guilt and shame too long. Jennifer told me it was time to move forward and to trust God. He brought Joshua into my life.*

"Let's pray," Joshua said. He took Mandy by the hand and prayed. As he prayed a peace fell over Mandy like a gentle, cool rain. She felt surrounded by the love of God.

"Mandy, I know God didn't bring me all the way out here to California just to be the youth pastor. He brought me here to find you and make you my wife. I've prayed all my life for God to bring me the wife He chose for me—and here you are."

She threw her arms around Joshua. "Yes! Yes. I'll marry you."

≈31≈

They decided on a December wedding. It was what she always dreamed of. The altar and the walls of the church were lined with red and white poinsettias. Allie had put four Christmas trees in the front of the church, which she decorated with white lights. Mandy chose a winter-white velvet wedding dress. She picked out green velvet dresses for her bridesmaids. Allie looked stunning in her red velvet gown. All the men in the wedding party had on black tuxedos with green ties. They wore red carnations in their lapels. Mandy's bouquet consisted of gardenias and red roses.

She and Joshua found the perfect wedding party gift. It was a wood slice candle holder. A bunch of red and pink dried flowers were tied with jute twine and attached was a heart containing the names of the bride and groom and their wedding date.

Jennifer Riggs came from Idaho to be Mandy's maid of honor. For a wedding gift she bought Mandy and Joshua a mountain scene throw blanket with their names and wedding date on it.

"I love this, Jennifer. It's perfect."

Joshua's parents gave the couple the down payment on a two-bedroom cabin. The best thing about this cabin was that it was on Gilner Point, just blocks away from Mandy's mom. Allie and Pastor Tom gave them money to buy furniture.

Joshua's father rented Wyatt's restaurant at the convention center for the reception. Allie's sister, Amy, decorated the room with white tablecloths. Each table had a vase of red roses and silver candlesticks. Each one either held a red or green candle. The room had streamers of white lights hung from the ceiling. The dinner entree was a choice of beef well-ington or risotto with winter greens.

Ben, Mandy's uncle, gave her away. When Mandy walked down the aisle, Joshua held his breath. He had never seen anyone so beautiful. Mandy looked at him. Her heart was about to burst. Mandy and Joshua stood under an arch. White, sheer material was draped over and lit with white lights and an artificial peony vine.

Pastor Tom performed the ceremony. Joshua and Mandy had written their own vows. Mandy went first. "Joshua, I love you. Long ago you were just a dream and a prayer. This day, like a dream come true, the Lord Himself has answered that prayer. For today, Joshua, you, as my joy, become my crown. I thank Jesus for the honor of going through life with you. With our future as bright as the promises of God, I will care for you and honor you. You are my friend and my love. Today I give myself to you."

Joshua had tears in his eyes as he proceeded with his vows. "I love you, Amanda Joy. You are my joy. I know God has ordained this love. Because of this I desire to be your hus-band. Together we will be vessels for His service in accor-dance with His plan, so that in all areas of our life Christ will have the pre-eminence. I promise to be faithful to you. I promise to love, guide, and protect you as Christ does His church, as long as we both are alive. According to Ephesians 5, and with His enabling power, I promise to endeavor to show to you the same kind of love as Christ showed the Church when He died for her, and to love you as a part of myself because in His sight we shall be one."

The joy Mandy felt she knew came only from being in God's perfect will for her life. She looked over at Allie and smiled. Her mother was wiping her eyes. Mandy knew they were tears of joy.

Before Pastor Tom told Joshua to kiss his bride, he asked the couple to turn around and face the congregation. "I'd like you all to join me in celebrating this marriage. I now introduce to you Pastors Joshua and Amanda Savage."

Everyone clapped.

"Now, Joshua, you may kiss your bride."

Discussion Questions
for *The Christmas Welcome Sign*

Use these questions for individual reflection or discussion in a book club or small group. They will help you not only understand some of the issues in *The Christmas Welcome Sign* but also integrate some of the book's messages into your own life.

1. What things did Allie do to strengthen the mother-daughter relationship between her and Mandy?

2. What behaviors in Logan did Allie recognize caused her to be concerned for her daughter?

3. Explain how Logan Walker was a master manipulator.

4. Mandy allowed herself to live in condemnation. Who is the one who condemns us? How do we know that Christ doesn't condemn us?

5. Jennifer was a good friend to Mandy. She told her the truth about her relationship with Logan, even risking losing their friendship. Have you ever had a friend like Jennifer? Share about it.

6. What ultimately caused Mandy to leave Logan? Was there anything else other than his actions?

7. In what way did Mandy lose her first love? Read Revelation 2:4 in the *Amplified Bible*. What is the danger of putting someone else first in your life other than Christ? How did Mandy restore her relationship with Christ?

8. Did Allie trust God to bring her daughter home? If your answer was yes, describe how you know that.

9. Romans 8:28 promises us that all things work

together for good to them that love God. Explain how the story testifies to this.

10. Compare and contrast with the parable of the prodigal son.

11. In Jeremiah 29:11 the Lord declares, "For I know the plans I have for you, plans to prosper you and not to harm you, plans to give you a hope and a future."

How does that hold true in the statement Joshua Savage makes: "God didn't bring me here just to be the youth pastor."

12. What is the significance of Pastor Tom telling Mandy and Joshua to turn around and face the congregation and then introduces them as Pastors Amanda and Joshua Savage?

About the Author

DEJAH EDWARDS is a respected author and inspirational speaker. She has earned a Master's degree in both biblical counseling and education. She is the author of the fiction books *Shattered Innocence A Journey To Restoration* and *Mama I Want To Be Like You*, and the nonfiction books *Honor Yourself You Are Highly Favored and Loved* and *God's Lent Child.*

She writes from her own personal experiences with abuse, rejection, and disappointment. But she knows a God who loves unconditionally and desires to restore the broken pieces of a life. Her passion is to bring hope and healing to women of all ages through her writing. Dejah, her husband, Ron, and their three dogs live in Yucaipa, California.

Contact Information

Dejah Edwards would love to hear from her readers. If you would like to send a comment, contact her to book a speaking engagement, or to order more copies of this book, email her at: Dejah05@gmail.com or you can visit her website: www.deeplylovedbyHim.com